For my dad

and Tom, Chester, Blackie, Mitzi,
Bagpuss, and Alfred

Atheneum Books for Young Readers
An imprint of Simon & Schuster Children's Publishing Division
1230 Avenue of the Americas
New York, New York 10020

Originally published in Great Britain in 2006 by Orchard Books
Published by arrangement with Orchard Books
The text for this book is set in Steam.
Manufactured in Mexico
First U.S. Edition 2007
4 6 8 10 9 7 5 3

Library of Congress Cataloging-in-Publication Data
Lloyd, Sam.
Mr. Pusskins : a love story / written and illustrated by Sam Lloyd.—1st ed.
p.   cm.
Summary: Grumpy Mr. Pusskins hates doing ordinary cat things such as playing with his owner Emily but a night out on the streets in search of
adventure makes him reconsider the advantages of a loving home.
ISBN-13: 978-1-4169-2517-0
ISBN-10: 1-4169-2517-1
[1. Cats—Fiction.] I. Title: Mister Pusskins. II. Title.
PZ7.L77875Mr 2007
[E]—dc22   2005030602

Mr. Pusskins
a love story

Written and illustrated by

sam lloyd

Atheneum Books for Young Readers

New York London Toronto Sydney

This is the story of a little girl called Emily and her dear cat, Mr. Pusskins.

Emily adored Mr. Pusskins.

Each morning
she would invent
fun games for
Mr. Pusskins to play.

In the afternoons
she'd brush his long
fur coat and tell him,

"Oh, Mr. Pusskins, what a handsome boy you are!
I **do** love you ever so much."

And each night Emily would snuggle up in bed and read Mr. Pusskins a special story.

But Mr. Pusskins
never listened.

The girl's constant babbling,

"Blah~de~blah, blah, blah,"

bored his whiskers off.
He wanted more than this dull life.

He went places he **wasn't** meant to go

and did things he **wasn't** meant to do,

and made friends with the **Pesky Cat Gang.**

such naughty fun!

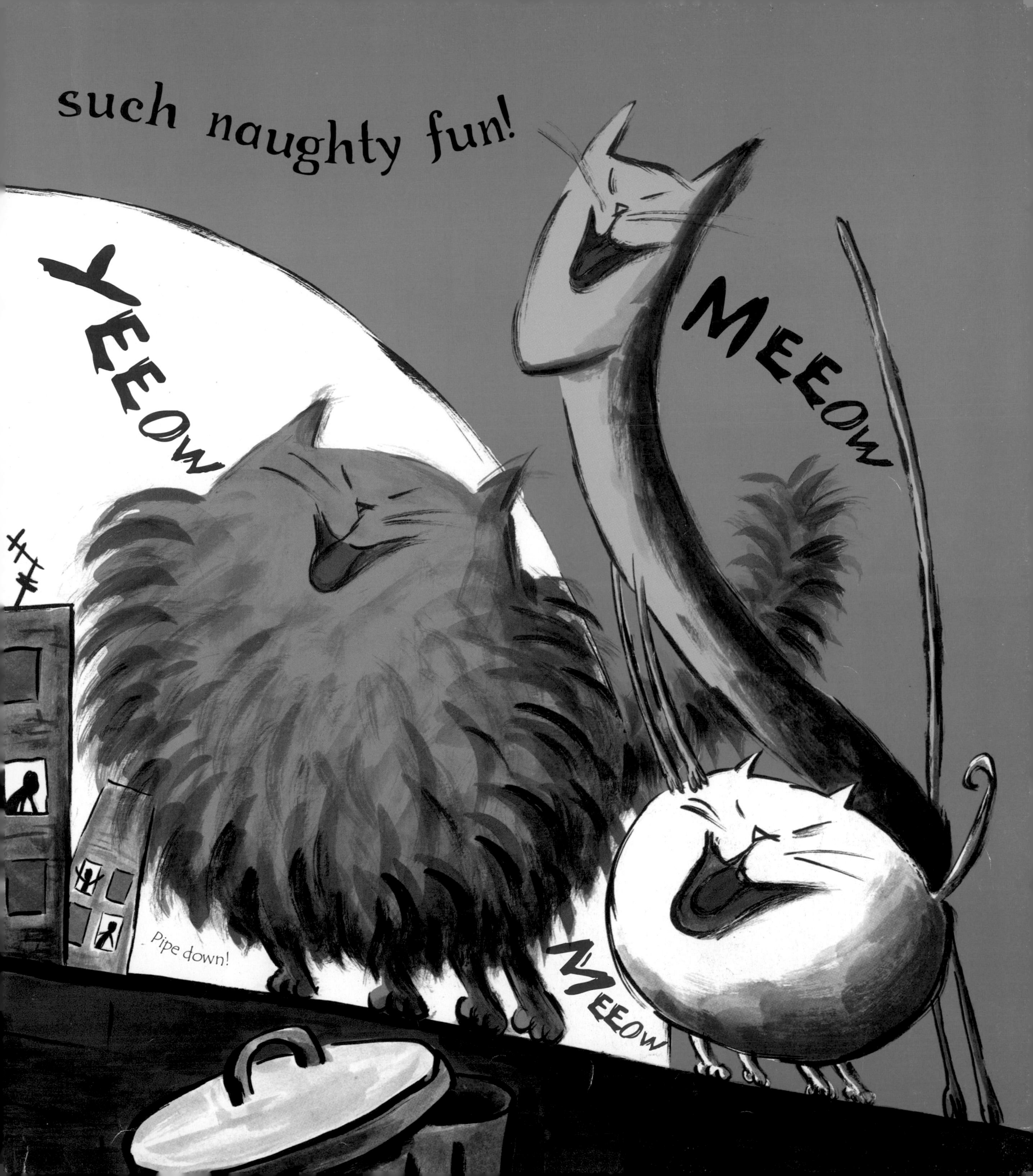

But time passed and things **changed**.
The rain fell and an icy wind blew.

The things Mr. Pusskins wasn't supposed
to do weren't fun anymore. And his new
friends weren't really very nice.

How lovely it would be to
have someone brush his fur
and tell him how much they loved him.

He felt all **alone.**

Then down the gray streets fluttered a tatty, old poster. It was a picture of Mr. Pusskins!

LOST:
mr. pusskins
Phone: 693900

LOST:
mr. Pusskins
Phone: 693900

LOST:
mr. Pusskins
Phone: 693900

He stared at the photo.
What a bad-tempered cat he looked.
Emily had given him **everything**
a cat could ever dream of . . .

LOST
mr. Pusskins
Phone:

but he had
never been nice to her.

How
sorry
he felt.

Mr. Pusskins found a phone.
He dialed the number from the
poster and waited anxiously.

Someone answered!

"Meow," whimpered Mr. Pusskins in a very sad little voice.

"Mr. Pusskins! Is that you? Oh, thank goodness," said Emily. "Wait there, I'll come and get you!"

Mr. Pusskins sat patiently.

Would Emily **find** him?

Did she still **love** him?

He waited
and **waited**.
But Emily didn't come.

Then, from over the mountains, he heard a car. Mr. Pusskins's heart leapt!

It was Emily! His dear Emily was coming for him!

. . . the car screeched to a halt and Emily jumped out. "Mr. Pusskins! My **beautiful** Mr. Pusskins!" she cried. "I didn't recognize you!"

Emily scooped up her dear cat.
At last they were

together
again.

This is the end of the story of a little girl called Emily and her dear cat, Mr. Pusskins.

Mr. Pusskins **adores** Emily.

Every evening, he cuddles her

and **purrs** gently while she reads to him.

Now both Emily and Mr. Pusskins realize how lucky they are to have **each other**.